spot

AFRICAN ANIMALS

ELEPHANTS

by Mary Ellen Klukow

AMICUS | AMICUS INK

trunk

tusks

Look for these words and pictures as you read.

tail

ear

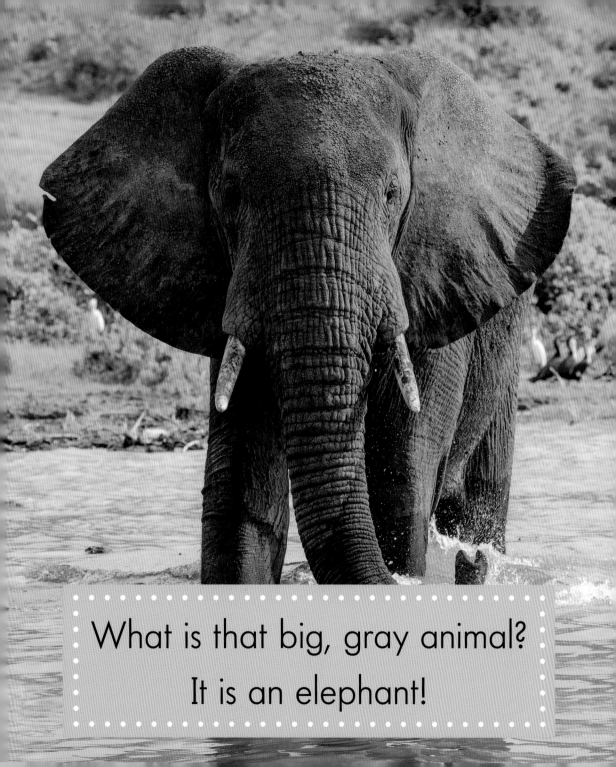

What is that big, gray animal?

It is an elephant!

An elephant lives with her family.
It is called a herd.
They find plants to eat.

Do you see the trunk?
It is long.
It can grab food.

trunk

tusks

Do you see the tusks?

Baby elephants lose their first tusks.

Then they grow new ones.

Do you see the tail?
Swish!
It scares off flies.

tail

ear

Do you see the ears?
They help the elephant stay cool.
It is hot on the savanna.

An elephant finds a puddle.
He calls to his mother.
Time to play!

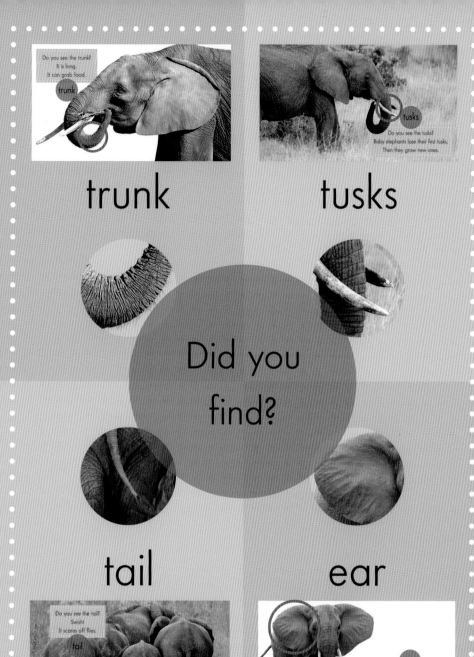

trunk

tusks

Did you find?

tail

ear

Spot is published by Amicus and Amicus Ink
P.O. Box 1329, Mankato, MN 56002
www.amicuspublishing.us

Library of Congress Cataloging-in-Publication Data
Names: Klukow, Mary Ellen, author.
Title: Elephants / by Mary Ellen Klukow.
Description: Mankato, Minnesota : Amicus, [2020] |
    Series: Spot. African animals | Audience: K to Grade 3.
Identifiers: LCCN 2018025815 (print) | LCCN 2018031222
    (ebook) | ISBN 9781681517209 (pdf) | ISBN
    9781681516387 (library binding) | ISBN 9781681524245
    (paperback) | ISBN 9781681517209 (ebook)
Subjects: LCSH: Elephants--Africa--Juvenile literature.
Classification: LCC QL737.P98 (ebook) | LCC QL737.P98
    K525 2020 (print) | DDC 599.67--dc23
LC record available at https://lccn.loc.gov/2018025815

Printed in China

HC 10 9 8 7 6 5 4 3 2 1
PB 10 9 8 7 6 5 4 3 2 1

Wendy Dieker, editor
Deb Miner, series designer
Ciara Beitlich, book designer
Holly Young, photo researcher

Photos by Shutterstock/Talvi cover;
Shutterstock/cyo bo 1; iStock/ChrisMajors
3; Getty/Manoj Shah 4–5; Alamy/
Volodymyr Burdiak 6–7; iStock/Musat
8–9; iStock/AOosthuizen 10–11; iStock/
bucky_za 12–13; iStock/anzeletti 14

ELEPHANTS